Footsteps of the past

G000082697

John Bunyan

The story of how a hooligan and soldier became a preacher, prisoner and famous writer

ANDREW EDWARDS AND FLEUR THORNTON

········ SEE **TRAVEL WITH JOHN BUNYAN** PA

A narrow escape

ately, things only got worse fo

from a bad attac

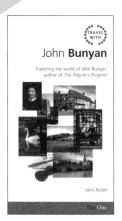

TRAVEL WITH

John **Bunyan**

Exploring the world of John Bunyan, author of *The Pilgrim's Progress*

John Pestell

Day One

LOOK OUT FOR THIS!

Throughout the book you will see this at the top of each page. If you have a copy of *Travel with John Bunyan* it will help you to explore the story of Bunyan in more detail— but it is not essential.

Travel with John Bunyan is available from Day One Publications.

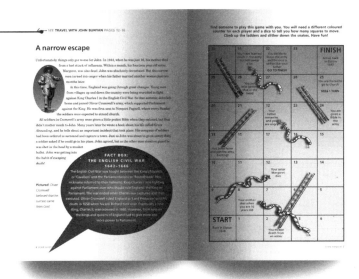

DayOne

Meet John Bunyan

From a poor, unknown family, mending pots by day and getting into trouble with local gangs by night, John Bunyan ended up in prison – but for a very different reason. He is now one of the best known authors of all time.

Question 1
Would you be prepared to spend twelve years of your life in prison for something you believed in?

Question 2
How did one game on the local playing field change his life for ever?

Question 3
Why did John Bunyan's wife storm the local pub?

Question 4
How many times can one man escape death?

Read on to find the answers …

'John, are you mad?'

'What are you doing? Are you mad? Leave it alone!'

The boy looked on in horror as John stepped forward. The two friends had been strolling through a field when an adder slid right across the track in front of them. John immediately grabbed a stick and struck the snake on its back. The adder lay there, stunned. Without stopping to think, John opened its mouth and plucked out its poison with his bare hands. This was not the only time John had a near-death experience.

John Bunyan was born in 1628 in a cottage in the tiny village of Harrowden, near Elstow just south of Bedford. He had a younger brother and sister—William and Margaret. His mother's name was also Margaret, and his father, Thomas, was a tinker, or tinsmith, who travelled from house to house mending pots and pans. It was not a well paid job, so money was often scarce.

As a child, John was sent to school, although he admits, 'I soon lost the little that I learnt' – does that sound familiar?

By the time John was nine or ten he was often found roaming the area with his friends: swearing and getting into trouble. He hated having to go to church on Sunday as it reminded him of the bad things he had done during the week. He just wished God would leave him alone.

Pictured above right: *All that remains of the place of John Bunyan's birth is a plaque etched onto a large slab of stone in a cornfield.*

Pictured top: *A drawing of the cottage Bunyan was born in.*

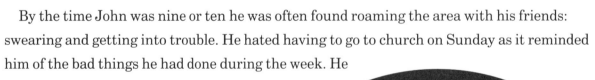

FACT BOX:
John Bunyan's family history in Bedfordshire went back a long way. People with that name are known to have lived near Harrowden since 1199. But until the eighteenth century there was no right and wrong spelling, and the name Bunyan is spelt thirty different ways in ancient records.

As you read this chapter, read the questions on the snake and write your answers on the lines provided.

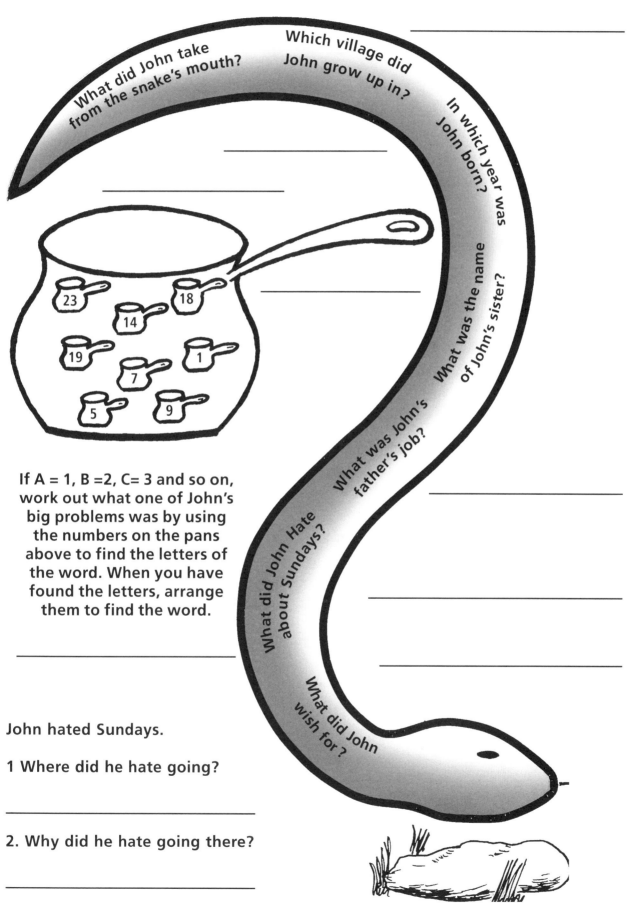

What did John take from the snake's mouth?

Which village did John grow up in?

In which year was John born?

What was the name of John's sister?

What was John's father's job?

What did John Hate about Sundays?

What did John wish for?

If A = 1, B =2, C= 3 and so on, work out what one of John's big problems was by using the numbers on the pans above to find the letters of the word. When you have found the letters, arrange them to find the word.

John hated Sundays.

1 Where did he hate going?

2. Why did he hate going there?

A narrow escape

Unfortunately, things only got worse for John. In 1644, when he was just 16, his mother died from a bad attack of influenza. Within a month, his fourteen year old sister, Margaret, was also dead. John was absolutely devastated. But this sorrow soon turned into anger when his father married another woman just two months later.

At this time, England was going through great changes. Young men from villages up and down the country were being recruited to fight against King Charles I in the English Civil War. So that summer, John left home and joined Oliver Cromwell's army, which supported Parliament against the King. He was first sent to Newport Pagnell, where every Sunday the soldiers were expected to attend church.

All soldiers in Cromwell's army were given a little pocket Bible when they enlisted, but that didn't matter much to John. Many years later he wrote a book about his life called *Grace Abounding*, and he tells about an important incident that took place. His company of soldiers had been ordered to surround and capture a town. Just as John was about to go on sentry duty, a soldier asked if he could go in his place. John agreed, but as the other man stood on guard he was shot in the head by a musket bullet. John was getting into the habit of escaping death!

Pictured: Oliver Cromwell believed that his success came from God.

FACT BOX: THE ENGLISH CIVIL WAR 1642–1646

The English Civil War was fought between the King's Royalists or 'Cavaliers' and the Parliamentarians or 'Roundheads' (this nickname referred to their helmets). King Charles I was fighting against Parliament over who should rule England: the King or Parliament. The war ended when Charles was captured and then executed. Oliver Cromwell ruled England as 'Lord Protector' until his death in 1658 when his son Richard took over. Eventually a new King, Charles II, was crowned in 1660. However, from now on the kings and queens of England had to give more and more power to Parliament.

Find someone to play this game with you. You will need a different coloured counter for each player and a dice to tell you how many squares to move. Climb up the ladders and slither down the snakes. Have fun!

30	31 You have learnt much in the army but still swear a lot	32 You decide to leave the army and become a tinker like your father **GO TO FINISH**	33	**FINISH** Arrive back in Elstow 1647
29	28 You just miss getting shot in the head	27	26	25 You are forced to go to church **MISS 1 TURN**
20	21	22 Your father remarries and you are angry	23	24 You are given a Bible in the army
19 You leave home and join the army. Exciting!	18	17	16	15
10	11	12 Your sister Margaret dies	13	14
9	8 Your mother dies when you are 16 years old	7	6	5
START Born in Elstow 1628	1	2 You escape death from an adder	3	4

❖•••••• SEE **TRAVEL WITH JOHN BUNYAN** PAGES 27–29

Two-faced

John took a deep breath as he strolled down the familiar tracks leading to Elstow. Little had changed in the three years he had been away fighting. He had gone away to war as a boy and now he returned as a man. By the time he was twenty-one years old, just two years later, John married a local girl and they lived in a cottage in the nearby village of Elstow. John and his wife

were so poor that he wrote: 'We came together as poor as poor might be, not having so much household stuff as a dish or spoon between us both.' Apart from fighting, John only knew one trade. So, following in his father's footsteps, he went back to working as a tinker: mending pots and pans.

But John was leading a double life. On Sundays he would go regularly to church with his wife. When she got married, her father had given her two Christian books— which she often read to John. But he was two-faced: he would sing and say the right things to please his wife, yet some of his actions showed he did not mean it.

The sermons John heard from the Puritan preacher Christopher Hall at Elstow church often worried him, but once he had eaten his Sunday lunch he soon forgot all about the sermon and would join his friends on the village green. John was known in the area for his swearing and lying and he quickly slotted back into becoming the ringleader of the local gangs.

**FACT BOX:
THE PURITANS**
The Puritans were Christians who believed the Bible was true and that it should govern every part of life. They had very strict moral standards. Most of the Puritans were on the side of Parliament in the Civil War. Their aim was to try and make the nation and the Church of England follow exactly the teaching of the Bible.

Pictured top: *The cottage in Elstow where Bunyan and his wife lived. It was pulled down for road widening in 1968.*
Pictured above: *The Moot Hall in Elstow, a building that John would have known.*

Describe John's life as a young man when he returned to Elstow in 1647.

_____

_____

_____

_____

_____

John was still the leader of the local youth gangs. Use coloured pencils or pens to produce graffiti for John and his gang.

Draw a picture of John and his new wife Mary at the age of 21.

John was described as leading a double life?

Why was this?

THINK!!

Are you doing anything secret in your life that other people might think means that YOU are living a double life?

Close encounter

Life was great: John had a wife, a home, friends and a job. But things were never that simple for him. One Sunday he was sitting in church listening to Christopher Hall preaching against people playing sports on Sundays. The problem was that John liked nothing better than playing on the village green on a Sunday afternoon. Did this mean that he was wrong? Was he wicked for having fun on a Sunday afternoon?

To get rid of these thoughts from his head, John went straight out after lunch that day and played tip-cat. He was just about to strike the 'cat' (not a real one!) when he heard a voice talking directly to him: 'What are you going to do? Leave your bad ways and go to heaven or keep your bad ways and go to hell?' John stopped immediately and stared up into heaven. Was God looking down on him right there? Could God see John's sinful life?

John did not know what was going on. In the days that followed he tried to carry on with his normal work, but everything he did seemed to make him think.

One day he was standing at a neighbour's shop window. As usual he began messing around and swearing so much that the shopkeeper came out: 'You are the most ungodly fellow that I have ever heard!' she said. Now this was saying something, as *she* had one of the foulest mouths in the village. But she didn't stop there; she was so shocked by what she had heard that she told John if he carried on, his language would affect all the young people in the area.

Pictured above: The anvil that John used in his work can be seen in the Bunyan Museum in Bedford. On one side there is an inscription 'J. BUNYAN' and on the other ' HELSTOWE 1647'.

**FACT BOX:
TIP-CAT**
Tip-cat was an old version of rounders.

John used to enjoy playing sports on the village green on Sunday afternoons but had felt 'challenged' by a sermon that it might be wrong.
Do you think it was wrong for him to play sports on Sundays or not? Why?

_____

_____

_____

_____

_____

_____

There are many people in history who have felt it was wrong to play professional sport on a Sunday because of what they believe.
Find out as much as you can about one such person.

Tip-Cat was an old form of rounders.

Design what you think a Tip-Cat court might look like.

▶

ALSO: make up some rules OR research how it was played.

▼

_____

_____

_____

_____

_____

The shopkeeper was worried that John's language and behaviour would affect the other young people in the village. Write one way on each ripple to show how this might happen. One has been done for you already.

Others might copy him

SEE TRAVEL WITH JOHN BUNYAN PAGES 37–38

Why me?

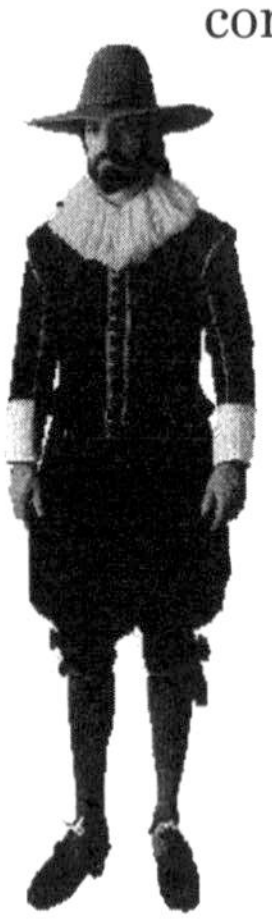

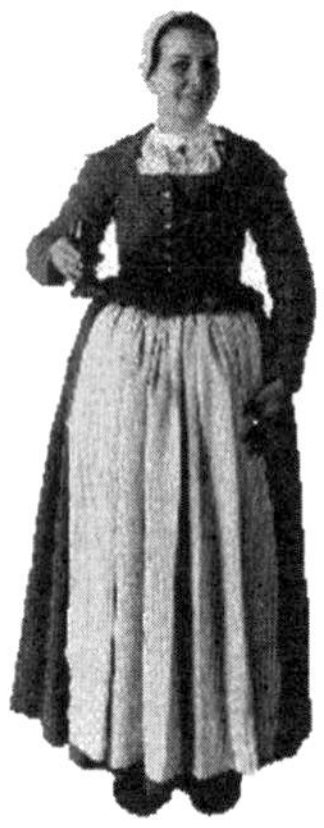

John started to question everything. One of his favourite pastimes was bell-ringing, but he began thinking, 'What's the point of it all?' He became so paranoid that one of the bells might come crashing down on his head, that he stood under the huge wooden beam of the steeple to protect himself. Later, he thought that a bell might hit him when it was swinging, so he moved to the steeple doorway. Eventually he thought the whole steeple might fall down on him, so he gave up bell-ringing altogether!

It didn't stop with bell-ringing either. John also gave up dancing, which was another of his favourite pastimes. What was going on? Why did he feel like this? Would God be pleased if he gave up all these things?

John and his wife had four children, but the first, called Mary, was born blind. Why had God let this happen?

John's life was changing. His friends could see it, his family could see it, but could God? Outwardly John was becoming very religious, but …

Pictured above: *This is the way people would have dressed in the seventeenth century.*

FACT BOX: VILLAGE LIFE IN THE TIME OF JOHN BUNYAN

John and Mary would have had very few belongings. Their clothes would have been made to last for many years and usually were in dark colours.

Follow the ropes to see which bell John rings.

Strange things were happening to John. In the story, what three things does it say happened that made him question God?

1. Divorced his wife ☐
2. Gave up bell ringing ☐
3. Bought a dog ☐
4. Child born blind ☐
5. Gave up dancing ☐
6. House burnt down ☐

This chapter finishes with the words: 'Outwardly John was becoming very religious, but...'
What do you think was the difference between what people saw outwardly and how John felt inside?

_____

_____

_____

_____

❖•••••• SEE **TRAVEL WITH JOHN BUNYAN** PAGES 39–40

Now I get it!

One day John was walking through Bedford town when he overheard a small group of women chatting as they sat in a doorway. They were talking about God – a subject John now felt he was a bit of an 'expert' in – so he thought he would listen in to their conversation. He soon realised by the way they were talking that they seemed to know God personally, and that troubled him even more.

John began to read the Bible as he had never read it before. He began pleading with God to show him what was really right. Was he a real Christian? John met up again with those women. They were among twelve members of a new church that had begun meeting in Bedford. So, each Sunday he went to St. John's where he slowly began to understand what God was saying to him through the Bible. At last, John realised that he needed to ask Christ to forgive his many sins. He later became a member of the church and was baptised, probably in 1653, in a little inlet of the River Ouse at Duck Mill.

On 14 April 1654 John and his wife had a daughter, Elizabeth. One year later the family moved to a very small, new home in Bedford. The house had just two rooms set either side of the front door. Over the fireplace of the room on the right, John carved his initials. This room became known as 'Bunyan's Parlour'.

Pictured top: This waterway is very near the site where John was baptised.

Pictured above: A plaque that marks the spot where John Bunyan was baptised. It reads: 'This backwater of the Great River Ouse is where John Bunyan was baptised circa 1650' (circa is a Latin word for 'about').

FACT BOX:
The baptism would probably have been conducted at night with lookouts posted to avoid arrest, because such meetings were illegal.

Write the answers to these clues in the grid above.

1. John had tried to follow these.
2. John eventually went to St. John's Church. He became one of these.
3. John's good------ wasn't so good.
4. This had been getting less.
5. John began to understand what this person was saying to him.
6. A group of women were sitting in this.
7. John started reading this like never before.

John prayed to God, asking God to show him what was the right and true way to live.
In the speech bubble, write the kind of prayer he may have said.

Answers:

1. Commandments
2. Member
3. Living
4. Swearing
5. God
6. Doorway
7. Bible

❖•••••• SEE **TRAVEL WITH JOHN BUNYAN** PAGES 45–49

Life changes

The change in John was amazing. In fact people were so impressed by it that they flocked to hear John Gifford, John's pastor at the church. Sadly Pastor Gifford died in September 1655. John was very upset. A new pastor, John Burton, was appointed in January 1656, but he was not a very healthy man.

About this time, John himself began preaching. He would often go with other preachers into the country to preach secretly. The members in his church soon recognised that John had a gift for this, and during 1656 they gave him permission to preach publicly.

John loved the Bible and was soon preaching in the open air, in houses, cottages, barns and even in parish churches. Crowds would gather to hear him. However, some unkind people thought that this tinker 'prated (that meant idle chatter) rather than preached.'

During the year, John and his wife had their third child, a son whom they named John. Two years later they had another son, and they called him Thomas. Life was as near perfect as it could be. Then disaster struck when his wife became ill. She became weaker and weaker until eventually she died. John was heartbroken. He had four children under ten years old, including one who was blind. What was he going to do?

His life had seemed so simple. He thought he had found out what God had wanted him to do with his life, but now he was not sure.

Pictured above: *This drawing is of John Bunyan preaching in October 1659. The small building in the distance is the town lock-up (or prison).*

FACT BOX:
JOHN GIFFORD

John Gifford had been an officer in the Civil War – on the opposite side to Bunyan! But like John, he was well known for swearing, drinking and gambling. Captured after a battle, he was going to be executed but his sister helped him to escape and he eventually worked as a doctor. When he became a Christian he began preaching and in 1650 became the first pastor of the church in Bedford which Bunyan attended.

Draw lines to match the people below with their place in the story so far, and find their names in the wordsearch.

D	U	S	A	G	S	D	W	O	R	C
J	B	P	X	L	P	Y	E	I	S	K
S	I	U	R	A	F	H	P	J	M	G
C	O	S	N	R	S	A	M	O	H	T
R	M	A	R	Y	W	E	L	H	O	J
O	J	A	F	X	A	R	P	N	R	A
L	T	F	T	O	H	N	F	V	O	N
W	A	F	E	S	P	H	I	M	Q	E
G	I	F	F	O	R	D	G	A	E	Z

Bunyan   The last child born to John and Mary

Gifford   The name of one of Bunyan's sons

Mary   The people who flocked to hear him preach

John   John Bunyan's pastor who died in 1655

Thomas   The main man in this story

Crowds   John Bunyan's wife who died

Colour this picture of John preaching

Imagine how John felt, left with his four young children after his wife died.

Write what he might have said in his diary.

Diary 1658

What things need changing in your life like those that changed in John's?

THINK!!

❖•••••• SEE TRAVEL WITH JOHN BUNYAN PAGE 49

Can't cope

Disaster after disaster struck. In September 1660 Pastor John Burton died, leaving the church without a leader. Worse still, the group of Christians then lost the use of the church building at St. John's. Now they had two major problems: no pastor and no building. They tried to make do by meeting in barns, stables and even cowsheds.

At home, John was very worried about his children. He just couldn't cope. He decided that he must find a wife, if only for the sake of the children. So, in 1660 he married Elizabeth, his second wife.

Oliver Cromwell, who fought against the king, had died in 1658 and Cromwell's son, Richard, took over the leadership of the country. However, Richard was not a strong leader and he lost most of the support that his father had gained, so he soon resigned.

Charles II was then invited to become the new king of England. As he stepped ashore at Dover, the new king announced that he loved the Bible more than anything else and that he would let people worship freely – but he soon forgot his promises. Crowds of people gathered on the roadside as he journeyed up to London. He arrived on 29 May 1660 – his thirtieth birthday.

Pictured above: Charles II became King in 1660 after Parliament failed to find a strong leader when Oliver Cromwell died.

FACT BOX: KING CHARLES II

The father of King Charles II had been executed at Whitehall in London in 1649. Charles then went to live in Europe for eight years until he was asked to become king. He was known as the 'Merry Monarch' because he let people play the games that the Puritans had banned.

BE A STORY DETECTIVE

What were the two problems for the church at St. John's?

1 _____

2 _____

What three places did they meet in?

3 _____

4 _____

5 _____

Who died in 1658?

8 _____

Who now became King?

9 _____

What happened in 1660 and why?

6 What? _____

7 Why? _____

On what date did this King arrive?

10 _____

What did he announce as he stepped ashore?

11 _____

_____

Check your answers. How many did you get right?

1. No pastor
2. No building
3. Barns
4. Stables
5. Cowsheds
6. Bunyan remarries
7. For the children's sake
8. Oliver Cromwell
9. Charles II
10. 29th May 1660
11. He loved the Bible

My score=____

1–5	Oops! Read it again. Sacked as a detective.
6–9	Not bad! You got to the bottom of it.
10–11	Super Sleuth! Well done!

Freedom?

The country was very pleased with their new king. A parliament was formed to try and get rid of Oliver Cromwell's followers because it didn't want any Puritans ruling the land, but John Bunyan was still excited about the future. The new king, Charles II, had declared he would let people worship as they wanted to. So things could not be too bad, could they?

John and his new wife Elizabeth were expecting their first child; the baby was due just before Christmas 1660. But as usual, life never seemed to go smoothly for John!

The magistrates at Bedford decided to enforce the Act of Uniformity which told everyone exactly how they were to worship God. John's small church refused to obey the law because they thought it was too much like the way the Roman Catholics worshipped.

The crunch came in November 1660 when John was asked to go and preach on a farm at Lower Samsell. He knew that he would be in danger if he went, but as he did not want to disappoint the people there, he went anyway. As soon as he arrived in the village, John was told that there was a warrant out for his arrest. What should he do?

Pictured above: *This is a picture of the Warrant for John's arrest in 1660.*

**FACT BOX:
THE ACT OF UNIFORMITY
1662**

In 1659 the King issued an Act of Parliament demanding that everyone should worship according to the Church of England Book of Common Prayer. In 1662 another Act of Uniformity reinforced this and as a result, over 2,000 ministers had to leave their churches because they refused to obey the law.

Wanted

Name _____

Why is he wanted? _____

_____

_____

_____

Where may he be found? _____

What may he be doing? _____

_____

_____

_____

_____

WHAT SHOULD HE DO?

Imagine you are John Bunyan. You are miles from home and about to do something illegal that God wants you to do. You hear there is a warrant for your arrest. What would you do and why?

_____

_____

_____

Find out more about the Puritans. What was life like for them and what exactly did they believe?

❖•••••• SEE **TRAVEL WITH JOHN BUNYAN** PAGES 58–61

Arrest!

When the people at Lower Samsell heard that John would be in danger if the meeting went ahead, they suggested that they should cancel it. John would not hear of it: 'Come, be of good cheer; let us not be daunted; our cause is good, we need not be ashamed of it; to preach God's word … even if we suffer for it.'

Just as the meeting was starting with prayer, a village constable burst into the house and ordered them to stop. A warrant was thrust into John's hands by the magistrate's assistant, who then arrested him. John was allowed to stay the night with a friend, who assured the magistrate that he would not escape. The next morning he was taken to Harlington Manor to face Judge Francis Wingate. Harlington Manor was a large house surrounded by a huge brick wall with enormous wooden gates at the entrance.

Without delay, John was taken to an oak panelled room where Wingate sat waiting for him. Wingate questioned him for most of the day. Each time, John responded calmly, but his answers were in vain. John's friends tried to come to his rescue, but Wingate was not prepared to listen.

John was then escorted twelve miles north to the county jail in Bedford's High Street to await sentencing.

Pictured top: John was questioned at Harlington Manor after his arrest.

Pictured above: The prison door from the county jail.

FACT BOX: BUNYAN'S PRISON CELL

The prison was on two levels. Two cells were below ground and one had no outside window. It did not have any fireplaces and the prisoners had to sleep on straw. One of its oak doors can be seen at the Bunyan Museum. See picture

Can you help John to get to the
meeting at Samsell Farm without
bumping into a constable (marked with
an x). If you do bump into a constable
by accident, go to the jail instead.
There are three ways he can go.
Can you find all three?

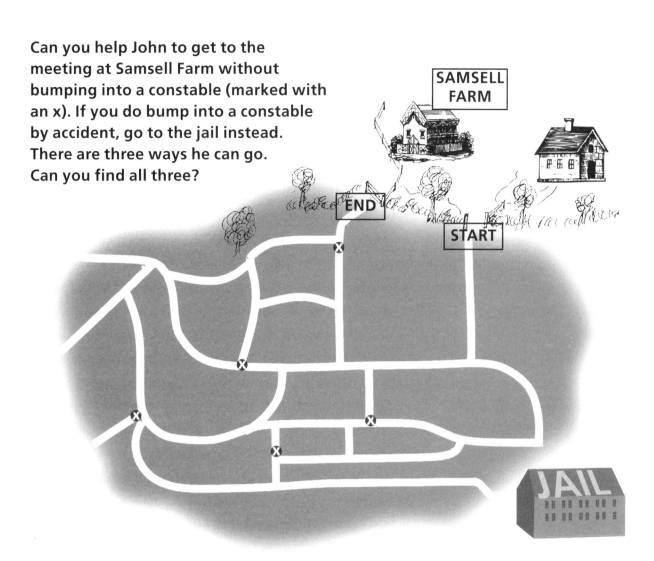

Write out two questions Wingate may have asked John, and John's replies:

QUESTION 1

Wingate's question: _____

John's reply: _____

_____

_____

QUESTION 2

Wingate's question: _____

John's reply: _____

_____

_____

Judgment

Another tragedy struck. John's family lived only five minutes from the jail. Elizabeth, who was expecting the birth of a baby within weeks, went into labour early and sadly the child was born dead.

John remained in prison for weeks before finally appearing before the County Court in January 1661. He was then taken to the Chapel of Herne, where he stood trial before five Royalist landowners; one of whom was Francis Wingate's uncle – hardly fair! The charge of leading unlawful meetings was read out.

John tried to defend himself by using verses from the Bible, but the men ordered,

'You must go back to prison, and stay there for three months … if you do not submit to go to church to hear divine service, *and stop your preaching* you must be banished from this country.'

And the judgment did not end there…

'If after that … you are found in this country without special licence from the King, you must stretch from the neck for it! (that meant hanged) – Take him away.'

As John was dragged away, he turned to the magistrate and said, 'Sir, as to this matter, I must argue with you; for if I am out of prison today; *I will preach the gospel again tomorrow – by the help of God.*'

Life in prison was hard, although his family was allowed to visit. Even blind Mary would go on her own to visit her father and take him some food.

After a while John was allowed out for a few hours at a time. John used this time to hold secret meetings until rewards were issued for information about them. He tried to use some of his time in prison by making leather laces for boots to raise money for his family as times were hard.

Pictured above: This is probably the very jug in which Mary took soup to her father.

**FACT BOX:
*THE PILGRIM'S PROGRESS***

Lord Hategood in Bunyan's famous book: *The Pilgrim's Progress* is based on the chief of the five landowners who gave judgement on John.

WAS IT WORTH IT?

Fill in the blanks from the words in the box below.

John's family lived five minutes from the _ _ _ _ that he was in. His wife went into early labour and his child was born _ _ _ _ . Eventually, in the month of _ _ _ _ _ _ _ , John went to court. Five wealthy landowners sentenced him to _ _ _ _ _ months in prison and banned him from ever preaching again. They said if he did, he would be 'banished from the _ _ _ _ _ _ _ ' and that if he was then caught, he would '_ _ _ _ _ _ _ from the _ _ _ _ for it. They then ordered 'Take him _ _ _ _ !'

ALL FOR PREACHING A SERMON!

jail	**January**	**country**	**neck**
	Stretch	**three**	**dead**	**away**

HANG IT ALL?

Trace the pieces of this hangman on to thick card, and cut them out. Colour each piece a different colour and number them.

Find a friend to play hangman with you, using the words on the right below, but don't let your friend know the words before you start.

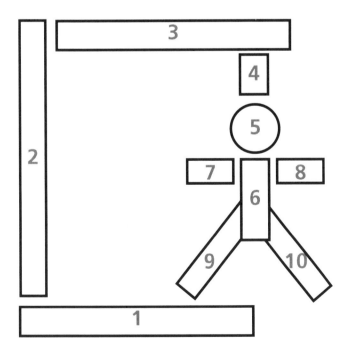

Wingate

Magistrate

Elizabeth

Herne

Unlawful

Prison

banished

hang

A B C D E F G H I J K L M N O P Q R S T U V W X Y Z

Elizabeth's fight for justice

Elizabeth and John drew up a petition for his release which Elizabeth took all the way to London. She spoke to an official in the House of Lords who told her John's only hope was at the hearing of the local Assize. This took place in August 1661 in front of two judges, one a Royalist, Sir Thomas Twisden, and a Lord from Cromwell's Parliament, Sir Matthew Hale. Hale received Elizabeth's petition, but was unsure what he could do.

The next day, as Twisden rode through the town in his coach, Elizabeth threw a copy of the petition through his open window and onto his lap. He was furious. He ordered the coach to

stop immediately and then shouted from his carriage that John would never be released until he gave up preaching. Later that day, during the court break, Elizabeth presented another copy of the petition to Matthew Hale. He began to read it until a local magistrate warned him not to.

So that was it. It seemed there was nothing else Elizabeth could do. But she had one more plan: she had heard that before leaving town, the judges would meet with the local landowners at the Swan Inn. Thinking only of her husband, Elizabeth pushed her way through the officials, climbed the stairs and entered the room. Raising her voice to speak over the noise, she spoke directly to the two judges: 'My husband has been falsely accused. He was not out to make trouble.'

She pleaded with them for John's release. But this time Elizabeth had tried the judges' patience too much. They demanded to know if he would give up his preaching. She replied, 'My Lord, he dares not leave preaching as long as he can speak.' Twisden ordered her from the room. Elizabeth left in tears and John remained in prison, on and off, for the next eleven years.

Pictured above: *Elizabeth pleading with Judge Twisden and Judge Hale, at the Assize, for her husband's release from prison.*

FACT BOX:
An 'Assize' is the court that meets regularly in every county in England and Wales to administer both civil and criminal law.

On four occasions Elzabeth tried to get her petition seen and her opinion heard. When were the four occasions?

1 _____

_____

2 _____

_____

3 _____

_____

4 _____

_____

In the speech bubbles, write the conversation Elizabeth had with the judge at the Swan Inn.

The Pilgrim's Progress

John did not waste his time in prison. He made bootlaces to help support his family, spoke to fellow prisoners about Jesus, and spent a lot of time writing. Before he had been imprisoned, he had already written nine different books and pamphlets. John wrote verse, rhyme, sermons, articles and stories. In 1666, the same year as the Great Fire of London, he wrote his own version of his life story called *Grace Abounding*.

John Bunyan's most famous book is the tale of *The Pilgrim's Progress*. It is the story of a journey taken by a man called Christian through this world to the next. On his action-packed journey from the City of Destruction, he meets many characters such as Mr. Worldly Wiseman, Charity, Faithful and Giant Despair. Some are there to encourage him on the right way, but others are there to persuade him off the right path. His adventures take him to many different places: The House Beautiful, the Valley of Humiliation and Doubting Castle. Eventually the pilgrim reaches the Celestial City.

The Pilgrim's Progress was a huge success. Within ten years of the first publication one hundred thousand copies had been printed. Even before John's death it was translated into several different languages.

Yet John did not receive much income from the sale of his books. When he died, his estate was worth no more than fifty pounds!

Eventually, during the spring of 1672, John was released from prison, but a few years later he was re-arrested. He remained in prison for another six months. During this time, his daughter Mary died at the age of eighteen, and his wife Elizabeth gave birth to a girl called Sarah.

FACT BOX:
THE INFLUENCE OF JOHN BUNYAN'S WRITING

John Bunyan wrote over sixty books or booklets during his lifetime. Two hundred years after his death it was said that almost every home in England had at least two books: a copy of the Bible and a copy of *The Pilgrim's Progress*. Today it is read all over the world in many languages. By the way, in those days fifty pounds would be more than the wages for a whole year of a working man.

Pictured above: *This is a sculpture of Christian fighting with Apollyon – a scene from The Pilgrim's Progress.*

This shows a stained glass window from the Bunyan Meeting Church in Bedford. Use the code at the bottom of the page to colour it in. Alternatively, trace it onto tracing paper and colour it using wax crayons to create one that can go on a window and will look like the real thing.

The window shows Bunyan in prison, writing.

BK = Black
BL = Blue
BR = Brown
G = Green

P = Purple
R = Red
W = White
Y = Yellow

Do not colour in his head or hands.

You may like to compare your finished picture with that on page 70 of *Travel with John Bunyan.*

❖•••••• SEE **TRAVEL WITH JOHN BUNYAN** PAGES 96–97, 100–101, 106–107

Free at last!

On 21 January 1672, while he was still in prison, John was appointed pastor to the Bedford Meeting, though the members had no building of their own. In May that year John was released from prison, now aged forty-three, and he received a licence to preach. A barn was

bought in Mill Lane so that the members could meet, although often the meeting took place outside due to the large numbers attending. In this year Elizabeth gave birth to a boy whom they named Joseph.

Finally, at the age of forty nine, John was released in 1677 after a second, short period in prison. Straight away he began travelling the area near Elstow to preach. He travelled on horseback, but had to be very careful to avoid robbers and highwaymen. At many crossroads stood a wooden frame on which criminals were hung by the neck to remind would-be robbers of their fate.

During the summer of 1688 John travelled to Reading in Berkshire, much against Elizabeth's wishes, as his health had been poor. During his journey back to London he was caught in a heavy storm and, exhausted and shivering with cold, he arrived at the home of his friend John Snow, a grocer in London. John went straight to bed with a hot drink of herbs. Three days later, feeling a little better, he preached in Whitechapel. But on the following Tuesday, John developed pneumonia. A doctor was sent for and he was nursed for the next ten days.

On Friday 31 August 1688, as the sun streamed through the bedroom window after a fierce thunderstorm, John summoned his friends to his bedside and whispered, 'Brothers, I desire nothing more than to be with Christ, which is far better.' He lifted his head slightly from his pillow and with arms outstretched cried, 'Take me for I come to thee!' And so, John Bunyan died at the age of sixty.

> **FACT BOX:**
> **JOHN'S FLUTE**
> Some think that John secretly made a flute out of one of the legs of his prison stool. Whenever the jailer came to investigate the noise John would return the flute to its original use on the stool! You can still see this flute in the John Bunyan Museum in Bedford.

John was buried on 3 September in Bunhill Fields in the City of London.

Pictured above: The tomb of John Bunyan in Bunhill Fields, a very old burial place in London.

Dates and numbers

Join each item in the left-hand column with a statement on the right-hand side that relates to it. One has already been done for you.

18 years old   John was released from prison for the first time

1668   The King declared himself a Catholic at this time

6 years   How old John was when he got a licence to preach

1672   The place John got to after being caught in a storm

21 January 1672   The age of Mary when she died

43 years old   The name of Elizabeth and John's son

Joseph   The date John was finally released from prison

1677   Where John went when he felt better

3000   How long John spent in prison the second time

1688   The date John officially became pastor in Bedford

Holborn   The number of people one Sunday who listened to John

Whitechapel   The year John was asked to solve an argument

3 September 1688   The date John died

31 August 1688   The date John was buried

Free at last!

At last John was free from jail. In his mind though, the real freedom came on 31 August 1688. Why do you think this was?

_____

_____

John Bunyan's Timeline

DATE	AGE	WHAT HAPPENED?
1628		John was born at Harrowden, near Elstow in Bedfordshire
1635		Royal Mail begins delivery
1642		The start of the English Civil War
1644	16	John's mother and sister died, and two months later his father remarried
1645	16	John joined Cromwell's army
1647	19	He returned home and became a tinker
1649	21	John married his first wife (we do not know her name).
1649		King Charles I was beheaded
1653	25	John heard a 'voice' whilst playing tip-cat and was later baptised in the river at Bedford
1656	28	John was appointed to preach, and published his first book
1658	30	John's wife died
1659	31	John married his second wife, Elizabeth
1660		Charles II was proclaimed King and passed the Act of Uniformity
1660	32	John was arrested
1665		The Great Plague in London occurred, which killed at least 70,000 people
1666		The Great Fire of London which destroyed 13,200 houses
1671	43	John was released from Bedford prison and later re-arrested He was appointed Pastor of Bedford Chapel
1675	47	John was finally released from prison
1675		Christopher Wren starts building St. Paul's Cathedral as we know it today
1680		Halley's comet is first discovered
1688	60	John died in London in the year that William of Orange came to the throne
1692		Elizabeth Bunyan died

© Day One Publications 2005   First printed 2005

A Catalogue record is held at The British Library   ISBN 1 903087 81 3

Published by Day One Publications Ryelands Road, Leominster, HR6 8NZ

☎ 01568 613 740 FAX 01568 611 473   email—sales@dayone.co.uk   www.dayone.co.uk   All rights reserved

*No part of this publication may be reproduced, or stored in a retrieval system, or transmitted, in any form or by any means, mechanical, electronic, photocopying, recording or otherwise, without the prior permission of Day One Publications. Unauthorised copying and distribution is prohibited.

Series Editor: Brian Edwards

Design and Art Direction: Steve Devane Thanks to Paul Sayer for his invaluable help with the artwork

Printed by Gutenberg Press, Malta

*Permission is given to copy the activity pages and associated text for use as class or group material